WALT DISNEY'S
DONALD DUCK'S
Toy Sailboat

TOLD BY ANNIE NORTH BEDFORD
PICTURES BY THE WALT DISNEY STUDIO
ADAPTED BY SAMUEL ARMSTRONG
FROM THE MOTION PICTURE "CHIPS AHOY"

GOLDEN PRESS
Western Publishing Company, Inc.
Racine, Wisconsin

This Little Golden Book was produced under the supervision of
THE WALT DISNEY STUDIO

Twelfth Printing, 1974

Copyright 1954 by Walt Disney Productions.
World rights reserved.
Produced in U.S.A. by Western Publishing Company, Inc.

"THERE!" said Donald Duck. "At last it's done!"
He stood back to look at his toy sailboat.
Making it had been a big job. It had taken
him all summer long. But now the boat was
finished. And it was a beautiful boat.

The mantel was just the place for it, too.
The whole room looked better with the sailboat up there.

"Building sailboats is hungry work," Donald
said to himself. So he fixed himself a fine big
lunch.

"Now to try out the boat in the lake," he thought. But his hard work had made him sleepy, too. So Donald settled down for a nap after lunch. After that he would try out the boat.

Now outside Donald's cottage in the old elm tree, lived two little chipmunks, Chip and Dale. And they had had no lunch at all.

"I'm hungry," said Chip, rubbing his empty middle.

"Me too," said little Dale. But suddenly he brightened. "Look!" he said.

Chip looked and looked. At last he spied it—one lone acorn still clinging to the bough of an oak down beside the lake.

Down the elm tree they raced, across to the oak, and up its rough-barked trunk.

"Mine!" cried Chip, reaching for the nut.

"I saw it first!" Dale cried.

So they pushed and they tugged and they tussled, until the acorn slipped through their fingers and fell *kerplunk* into the lake.

The two little chipmunks looked mighty sad as they watched the acorn float away. But Dale soon brightened. "Look!" he cried.

Chip looked. On a little island out in the middle of the lake stood a great big oak tree weighted down with acorns on every side.

Down to the shore the chipmunks ran. But br-r-r! It was too cold to swim.

"How can we get to them?" wondered Chip.

"I don't know," said Dale. But he soon had an idea. "Look in there!" he said.

On the mantel in Donald Duck's cottage they could see the toy sailboat.

"Come on," said Dale. So away they raced, straight in the cottage door.

They had the sailboat down and almost out
the door when Donald stirred in his sleep.
"Nice day for a sail," he said dreamily, as
the boat slipped smoothly past his eyes.

Soon after, Donald woke up completely.
"Now to try out my boat!" he cried.
Suddenly something outside the window
caught his eye. It was his sailboat, out on the
lake!

"I'll fix those chipmunks!" Donald said.
He pulled out his fishing rod and reel and
chose a painted fly. It looked just like a nut.
"This will do," Donald grinned.

From the pier he cast—as far as he could fling that little fishing fly. With a *plop* it landed beside the toy boat.

"Look! Look at this!" cried Dale. He leaned way over the edge of the boat to pull in the floating fly.

"Good! A nut!" said Chip. "We'll toss it in the hold and have it for supper tonight."

As soon as it was fast in the hold, Donald pulled in the line. He pulled that little boat right in shore. The chipmunks never suspected a thing. They did not even notice Donald pouring water into the cabin of the boat.

Chip discovered that when he went into the cabin. "Man the pumps!" he cried.

Those two chipmunks worked with might and main while Donald watched and laughed.

"Ha ha!" At Donald's chuckle, the chips looked up.

"So that's the trouble!" Dale cried.

He pulled out the fishing fly from the hold and flung it at Donald so that he was soon tangled up in fishing line.

While Donald tried to tug himself free, the chips set sail once more.

Before Donald could launch his swift canoe, they had touched at the island's shore.

As Donald was paddling briskly along, he heard a brisk *rat-a-tat-tat!*

The oak tree on the island seemed to shiver and shake as its store of acorns rained down.

The busy little chipmunks finished dancing on the branches. Then they hauled their harvest on board.

"Oh, well," said Donald, watching from his canoe. "At least I know the sailboat really will sail. Now let's just see what those little fellows do."

And can you guess what the chipmunks did? They stored their nuts in a hollow tree. And they took Donald's toy sailboat right back, and put it where it belonged!